T0387706

DAMS

by Catherine C. Finan

BEARPORT
PUBLISHING

Minneapolis, Minnesota

Bearport Publishing Company Product Development Team
President: Jen Jenson; Director of Product Development: Spencer Brinker; Senior Editor: Allison Juda; Editor: Charly Haley; Associate Editor: Naomi Reich; Senior Designer: Colin O'Dea; Associate Designer: Elena Klinkner; Product Development Assistant: Anita Stasson

Produced for Bearport Publishing by BlueAppleWorks Inc.
Managing Editor for BlueAppleWorks: Melissa McClellan
Art Director: T.J. Choleva
Photo Research: Jane Reid

Library of Congress Cataloging-in-Publication Data

Names: Finan, Catherine C., 1972- author.
Title: Dams / by Catherine C. Finan.
Description: Minneapolis, Minnesota : Bearport Publishing, [2023] |
    Series: X-treme facts. Engineering | Includes bibliographical
    references and index.
Identifiers: LCCN 2021061872 (print) | LCCN 2021061873 (ebook) | ISBN
    9798885091671 (library binding) | ISBN 9798885091749 (paperback) | ISBN
    9798885091817 (ebook)
Subjects: LCSH: Dams--Juvenile literature.
Classification: LCC TC541 .F56 2023 (print) | LCC TC541 (ebook) | DDC
    627/.8--dc23/eng/20220210
LC record available at https://lccn.loc.gov/2021061872
LC ebook record available at https://lccn.loc.gov/2021061873

For more information, write to Bearport Publishing, 5357 Penn Avenue South, Minneapolis, MN 55419. Printed in the United States of America.

Contents

Dams Can Do That! ... 4

A Long History ... 6

Built with Style ... 8

A Feat of Engineering ... 10

Hello, Hoover Dam! ... 12

A Grand Dam, Indeed ... 14

Up to the Challenge ... 16

A Dam on the Nile ... 18

Incredible Itaipú Dam ... 20

So Much Power! ... 22

Ready to Bungee Jump? ... 24

What Could Be Better? ... 26

Arch Dam ... 28

Glossary ... 30

Read More ... 31

Learn More Online ... 31

Index ... 32

About the Author ... 32

Dams Can Do That!

Imagine a structure so large and strong that it can block the flowing waters of a massive river and create a huge lake. That structure is a dam! Dams are marvels of **engineering** that hold back and store water. This water can be used for people to drink or to **irrigate** crops. It is even used to make electricity. Dams are amazing!

Beavers build little dams of sticks, rocks, and mud. **Humans basically stole their idea!**

There are about 60,000 large human-made dams around the world.

THEY KNOW A GOOD THING WHEN THEY SEE IT.

CAN'T THOSE HUMANS COME UP WITH THEIR OWN IDEAS?

OKAY, YOUR DAMS ARE NICE. BUT OURS ARE MUCH LARGER!

Dams create human-made lakes called reservoirs. Some people use reservoirs for fishing, boating, and swimming.

THIS DAM PRODUCES A LOT OF ELECTRICITY.

AWESOME! AND ITS RESERVOIR IS A GREAT PLACE TO GO FISHING!

Dams use water to make **hydroelectric** power, which provides about 16 percent of the world's electricity.

Water from dams is used to grow crops that feed about 15 percent of Earth's **population**. That's 1.2 billion people!

I'M NOT TRYING TO STEAL YOUR THUNDER, LADY LIBERTY.

DON'T WORRY, I'M NOT THE JEALOUS TYPE.

The Rogun Dam, which is under construction in Tajikistan, will be the world's tallest dam at 1,099 feet (335 m). **That's taller than the Statue of Liberty!**

A Long History

People have been building dams throughout history. Even the earliest dams, built thousands of years ago, were used to prevent floods, irrigate farmland, and store drinking water. These huge dams were built by hand, without the help of machines or computer technology. And some of these **ancient** dams are still in use today. Let's dig into the history of dams!

The oldest known dam, the Jawa Dam, was built about 5,500 years ago. Its **ruins** are in present-day Jordan.

I USED TO BE KIND OF A BIG DEAL.

The Saad-el-Kafara Dam contained 100,000 tons (90,718 t) of stone and gravel.

UGH, I KNOW! THIS DAM BETTER BE WORTH IT.

I CAN'T BELIEVE WE HAVE TO MOVE ALL THIS STUFF.

The ancient Egyptians built the large Saad-el-Kafara Dam in northwestern Egypt about 4,700 years ago.

The ancient Romans built the Cornalvo Dam in Spain about 2,000 years ago. It is still used today!

THAT'S WHAT I CALL SOME SOLID ENGINEERING.

YEAH, IT BRINGS BACK SO MANY MEMORIES!

Hundreds of years ago, small dams were built in Europe to power **paddle wheels**. These were used to grind grain and saw wood.

I DON'T WANT TO WORK ON THE DAMS!

About 3,000 workers built a set of dams in the Yangtze River basin in ancient China. The construction took nearly 10 years.

COME ON! THEY'LL ONLY TAKE 10 YEARS.

Built with Style

Today, there are a few main types of dams. An arch dam has a curved shape that holds back the water behind it while a gravity dam is usually built straight across a river valley. A buttress dam uses supports called buttresses to strengthen it. And an embankment dam is like a gravity dam, but it's made from natural materials. Although they all look a little different, most dams are made of **concrete** and have the same main parts. Let's check them out . . .

Arch Dam

Gravity Dam

Buttress Dam

Embankment Dam

The part of a dam that stretches along the top is called the crest.

LET'S TAKE A SELFIE WITH IT.

COOL CREST!

People can walk or drive on the crests of some dams.

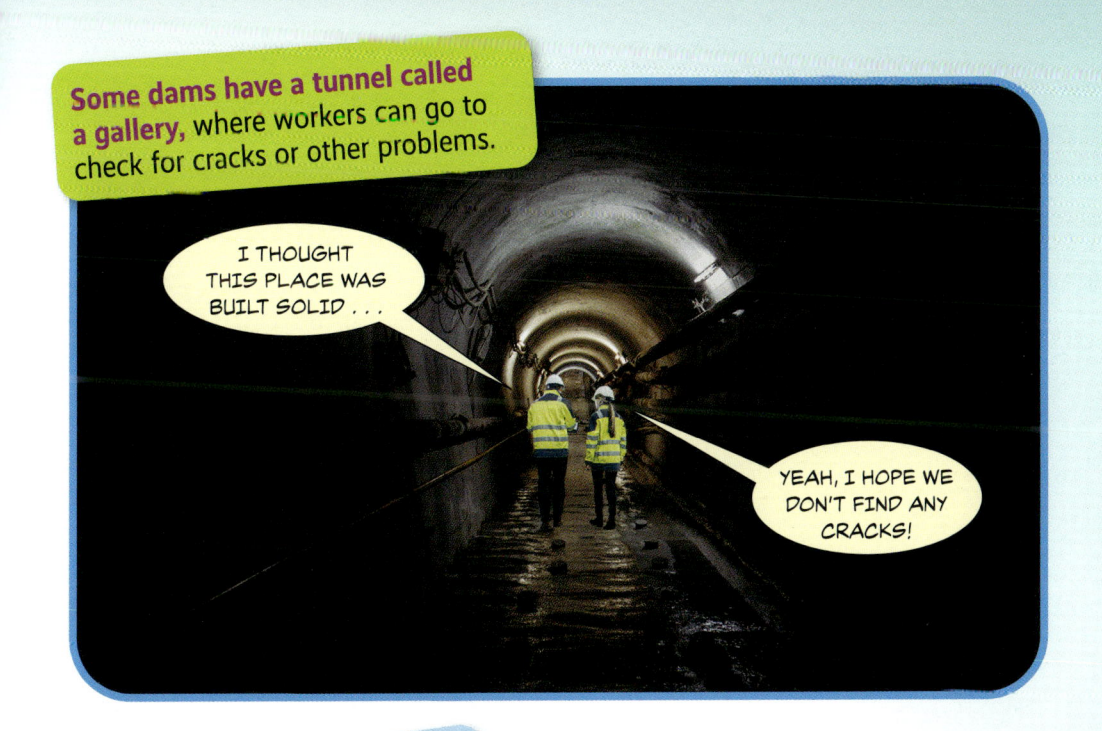

Some dams have a tunnel called a gallery, where workers can go to check for cracks or other problems.

I THOUGHT THIS PLACE WAS BUILT SOLID . . .

YEAH, I HOPE WE DON'T FIND ANY CRACKS!

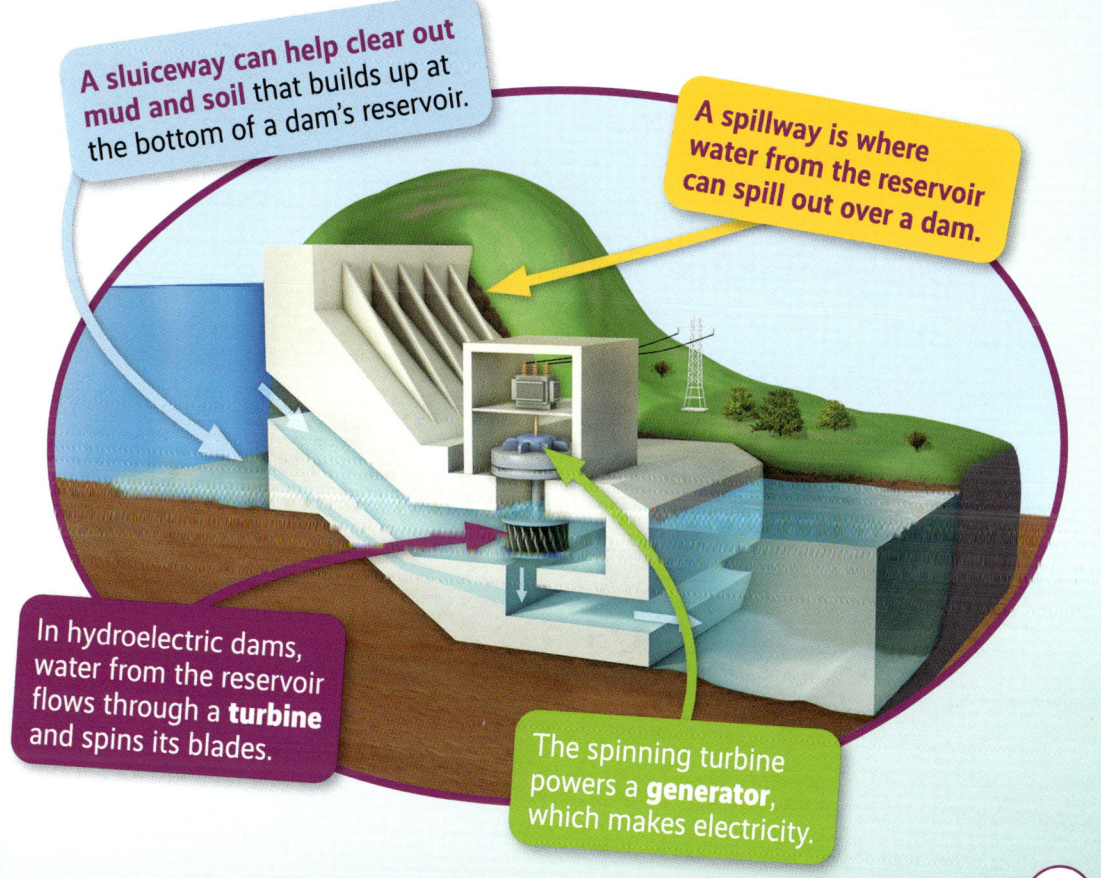

A sluiceway can help clear out mud and soil that builds up at the bottom of a dam's reservoir.

A spillway is where water from the reservoir can spill out over a dam.

In hydroelectric dams, water from the reservoir flows through a **turbine** and spins its blades.

The spinning turbine powers a **generator**, which makes electricity.

9

A Feat of Engineering

Whichever type it is, a dam must be strong enough to hold a huge amount of water in its reservoir. And making a structure that strong is not easy. The job takes planning, testing, and preparation. Once it's time to build, there's often another big challenge—changing the course of the river so construction can begin on dry land! Dams are amazing feats of engineering!

BRING ON THE WATER!

When a dam is being built on a small river, water is **diverted** through a tunnel or **channel** dug in soil and rock along the river's edge.

On a wide river, workers may block some water to build a dry construction pit on part of the riverbed. As they work, the river flows around them.

DOES THE WAY WE'VE BLOCKED THE WATER LOOK OKAY?

LOOKS GOOD FROM HERE!

Before construction starts, engineers take soil samples to make sure the ground is strong enough to support the dam's weight.

Weak soils or rocks found at the construction site are removed and replaced with stronger materials.

Most large dams are made with many tons of concrete. The concrete is poured into a huge frame made in the dam's shape.

Dams are built up gradually. The concrete is often added a few feet at a time. It's left to dry before more is added.

When a dam is finished, workers allow the river water to fill the reservoir. A job well done!

Hello, Hoover Dam!

Speaking of tons of concrete . . . When Hoover Dam was completed in 1936, it was the largest concrete structure in the world. Named after the 31st president of the United States, Herbert Hoover, this dam sits on the Colorado River along the border between Nevada and Arizona. It created Lake Mead, the largest reservoir in the United States. Today, millions of people visit the dam every year just to marvel at this example of excellent engineering!

During construction, not everyone was a fan of President Hoover. **Some people called the dam Boulder Dam until its name officially became Hoover Dam in 1947.**

Lake Mead provides Las Vegas, Nevada, with 90 percent of its drinking water.

So much concrete was used to build Hoover Dam that it **could have paved a road from New York City to San Francisco, California.**

San Francisco

New York City

I'VE GOT THE POWER!

Hoover Dam is a hydroelectric dam. It supplies power to about 1.3 million people each year.

Hoover Dam was such a huge project that an entire city—Boulder City, Nevada—**was built to house its thousands of construction workers.**

THIS IS HARD WORK!

Hoover Dam workers were paid between 50¢ and $1.25 per hour. In today's money, that would be between $9.50 and $24.00 per hour.

YEAH, BUT THE PAY IS GOOD.

A Grand Dam, Indeed

As the finishing touches were being put on Hoover Dam, another spectacular project was underway on the Columbia River in Washington State. When the Grand Coulee Dam opened in 1942, it beat out Hoover Dam as the largest concrete structure—with almost four times as much concrete! Today, electricity generated from the Grand Coulee Dam powers 4.2 million homes across 11 states and parts of Canada.

The Grand Coulee Dam is a gravity dam.

The amount of concrete used in the Grand Coulee Dam could make **a sidewalk long enough to wrap around Earth twice!**

YEAH, I AM COOL!

I'D SAY THIS DAM IS COOL-EE!

The dam is almost 1 mile (1.6 km) long and 550 ft (168 m) tall. **That's about three times the height of Niagara Falls.**

The Grand Coulee Dam's reservoir, Franklin D. Roosevelt Lake, is named after the 32nd president of the United States.

The dam itself gets its name from the area's deep valleys, or coulees, that were made by glaciers thousands of years ago.

This dam has openings big enough to drive a truck through. They let water out of the reservoir when the water cannot reach the dam's spillway.

The Grand Coulee Dam's base is almost four times as large as the base of Egypt's Great Pyramid.

Up to the Challenge

Building a dam sure is complicated. What about building one in a place far from towns and highways? That's an even bigger challenge! But Glen Canyon on the Colorado River in Arizona was the perfect place for a dam. The canyon's strong walls would help support the dam and reservoir. So, before construction on Glen Canyon Dam could begin in 1956, engineers had to figure out how to get supplies to this **remote** location. Let's see how it all turned out . . .

Glen Canyon Dam took seven years to build. It's the second-largest concrete arch dam in the United States.

A bridge was built across the canyon to get supplies to the construction site. This shortened the trip to the site from 200 miles (322 km) to just 0.25 miles (0.4 km)!

WHAT WOULD YOU PEOPLE DO WITHOUT ME?

THAT BRIDGE IS RATHER FULL OF ITSELF!

Glen Canyon Dam is 710 ft (216.4 m) tall. That's about the same as two football fields stacked end to end.

Once the dam was ready for its concrete to be placed, **people worked on it around the clock for more than three years!**

ARE WE ALMOST DONE HERE?

YUP, ONLY A FEW MILLION MORE TONS OF CONCRETE AND THEN WE CAN CALL IT QUITS!

About 9.6 million tn. (8.7 million t) of concrete were used to build Glen Canyon Dam.

The dam's reservoir, Lake Powell, was named after John Wesley Powell. He led the first successful boat trip down the Colorado River through the Grand Canyon.

WELL, I'M HONORED!

Lake Powell is the second-largest reservoir in the United States, after Hoover Dam's Lake Mead.

A Dam on the Nile

Can you imagine having to move an entire ancient temple complex—full of priceless stone statues—in order to build a dam? That's exactly what happened during the construction of the Aswan High Dam on the Nile River in southern Egypt. When the 2-mile (3.2-km) long dam was completed in 1970, it was considered one of the greatest engineering projects ever.

Abu Simbel was moved to higher ground, just 600 ft (183 m) west of the original site.

OOH, I LIKE THE VIEW FROM UP HERE!

I MISS OUR OLD SPOT!

Abu Simbel had sat in its original spot for more than 3,000 years.

The Aswan High Dam helps control the Nile River's flooding and provides hydroelectric power and irrigation.

About 90,000 people had to move away from their homes to make space for the Aswan High Dam's construction site.

HI, CROCODILES!

Nile crocodiles live in the dam's reservoir, Lake Nasser.

HELLO! WHAT DO YOU THINK OF OUR RESERVOIR? PRETTY NICE, RIGHT?

Incredible Itaipú Dam

Another one of the world's largest and most powerful hydroelectric dams is in South America. The Itaipú Dam is 5 miles (8 km) long, stretched across the Upper Paraná River between Paraguay and Brazil. It took 18 years to build—and almost 3 of those years were spent digging a channel for the river to flow through during construction. That's a lot of digging!

The Upper Paraná River is one of the largest rivers in the world. That's why diverting it during construction was not easy!

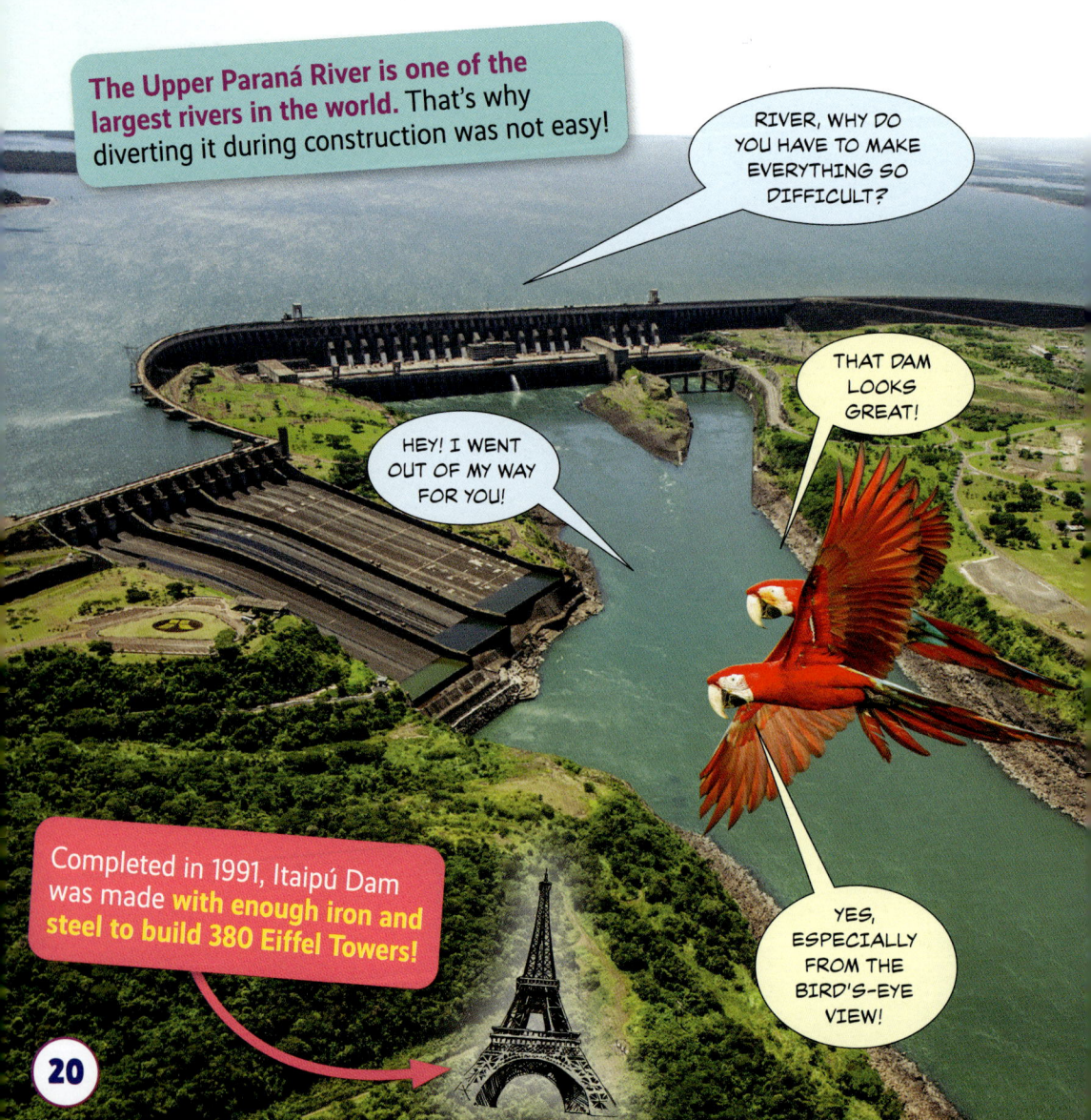

RIVER, WHY DO YOU HAVE TO MAKE EVERYTHING SO DIFFICULT?

THAT DAM LOOKS GREAT!

HEY! I WENT OUT OF MY WAY FOR YOU!

YES, ESPECIALLY FROM THE BIRD'S-EYE VIEW!

Completed in 1991, Itaipú Dam was made **with enough iron and steel to build 380 Eiffel Towers!**

About 50 million tn. (45 million t) of rock and dirt were moved while digging the channel to divert the river.

I CAN'T BELIEVE YOU HELPED MOVE ALL THOSE ROCKS!

YEP! IT WAS A LOT OF WORK.

Each year, the dam makes **more than 88 percent of the electricity used in Paraguay and 10 percent of the electricity used in Brazil.**

WELL, YOU DON'T HAVE TO BE SUCH A SHOW-OFF.

WOW, THAT'S SO MUCH ELECTRICITY . . . I'M SHOCKED!

At 643 ft (196 m) tall, **the dam is about the same height as a 65-story building.**

So Much Power!

While Itaipú Dam is big and powerful, the world's largest hydroelectric dam is actually Three Gorges Dam. This concrete gravity dam spans the Yangtze River near Yichang, China, and has a massive reservoir. Construction on this huge project began in 1994 and took about 30 years to complete. In 2020, the dam set a world record for most hydroelectric power produced in one year. Impressive!

Three Gorges Dam is 607 ft (185 m) tall. **That's taller than the Washington Monument!**

The reservoir created by the dam put 13 cities, 140 towns, and more than 1,600 villages underwater.

More than 1.3 million people had to move during construction because their homes were going to be covered by the dam and its reservoir.

The massive amount of water built up behind **the dam has actually slowed Earth's rotation by a tiny bit!**

I'M FEELING JUST A LITTLE BIT SLOWER THESE DAYS . . .

I'M SORRY! I'M TRYING TO HOLD BACK A LOT OF WATER.

The dam's system of **locks** allows large ships **to travel 1,400 miles (2,250 km) inland from the East China Sea.**

THAT'S A DOOZY OF A DAM!

WELL, GO BIG OR GO HOME.

23

Ready to Bungee Jump?

Dams are built for practical purposes—to produce power, control flooding, and provide water for millions of people. But they can also be used for very *non-practical* purposes, such as bungee jumping! The Contra Dam, a concrete arch dam on Switzerland's Verzasca River, was built to make electricity. However, its beautiful views and an appearance in a popular movie have turned the dam into a hot spot for bungee jumping!

The Contra Dam goes by a few names. Many people call it the Verzasca Dam. Some call it the Locarno Dam because it's near the city of Locarno.

HEY, WHO ARE YOU CALLING CHEAP?!

WHAT? I THOUGHT IT WAS JUST ONE OF YOUR MANY NAMES!

The Contra Dam has less concrete than typical arch dams. This made it cheaper to build.

The opening scene of the James Bond film *GoldenEye* features a dramatic bungee jump from the top of the Contra Dam.

THIS IS HOW JAMES BOND DID IT, RIGHT?

I THINK SO!

The Contra Dam is 720 ft (220 m) tall. Imagine bungee jumping from that height. *Yikes!*

When the dam's reservoir was filled, **the weight of the water caused earthquakes.**

YES, BUT AT LEAST WE'LL NEVER RUN OUT OF FRESH WATER!

IS YOUR HOUSE SHAKING, TOO?

THAT RESERVOIR IS NOTHING BUT TROUBLE!

What Could Be Better?

Throughout history, dams have played an important role in people's lives. As the world's population grows, so will the need for the water and electricity that dams can provide. But as dams get older, they can weaken, crumble, and rust. This can cause a dam to fail, putting people's lives at risk. The engineers of today—and tomorrow—must find ways to keep people and **environments** safe if they want to build dams that stand the test of time.

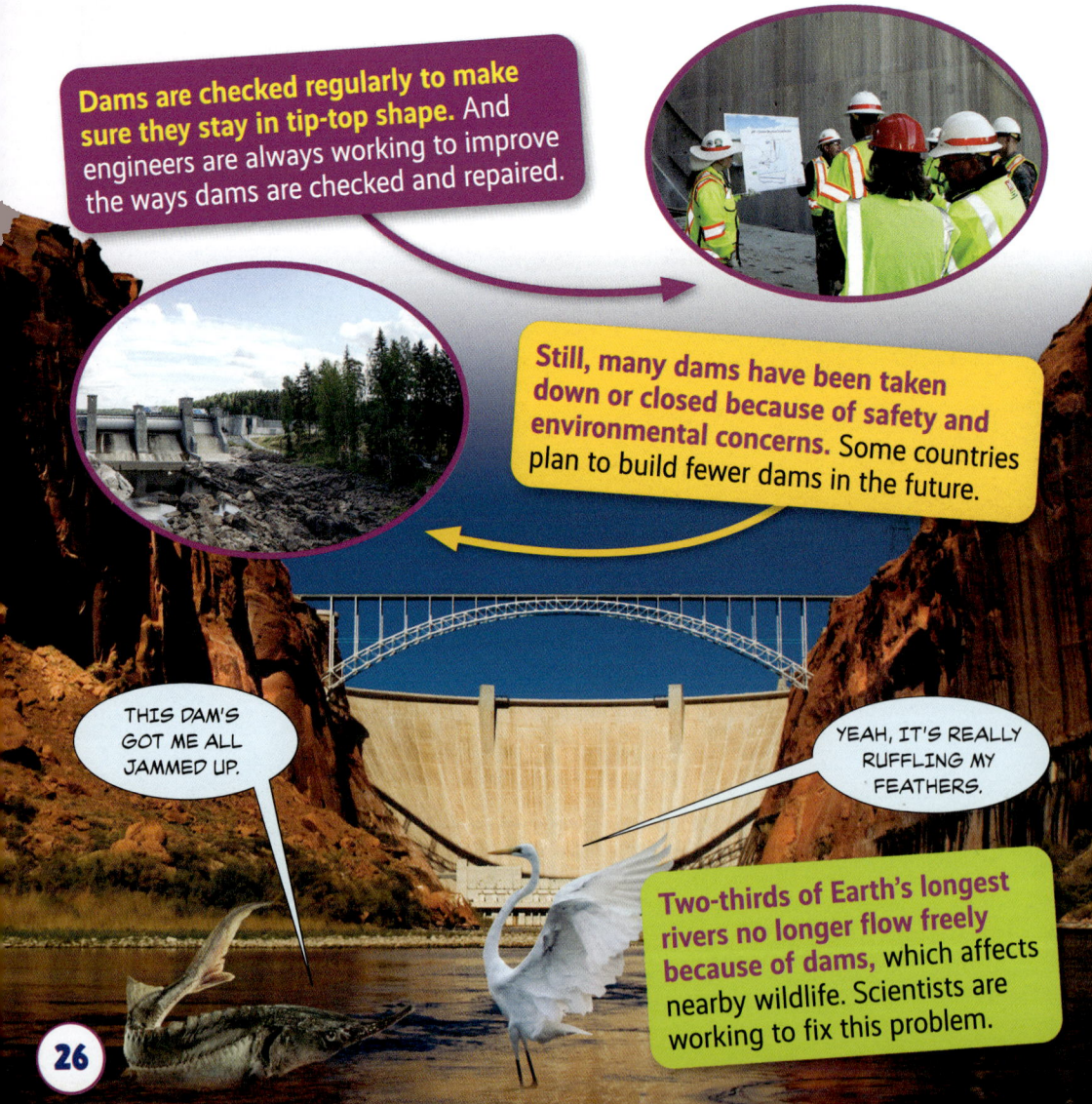

Dams are checked regularly to make sure they stay in tip-top shape. And engineers are always working to improve the ways dams are checked and repaired.

Still, many dams have been taken down or closed because of safety and environmental concerns. Some countries plan to build fewer dams in the future.

THIS DAM'S GOT ME ALL JAMMED UP.

YEAH, IT'S REALLY RUFFLING MY FEATHERS.

Two-thirds of Earth's longest rivers no longer flow freely because of dams, which affects nearby wildlife. Scientists are working to fix this problem.

Engineers are finding ways to make dams less harmful to fish. Some dams have fish ladders, which let fish move through places where a river is blocked.

WAIT FOR ME! THESE STEPS ARE RATHER STEEP!

HURRY UP! WE'RE ALMOST THROUGH THIS!

One company made a "salmon cannon" to help the fish get over tall dams. Salmon swim into a tube, and then the tube shoots them out over the dam.

WHAT A RIDE!

Some scientists are working to change the way water is released from dams so that it could be better for fish.

Arch Dam

Craft Project

Imagine you're an engineer and your job is to design a dam across a narrow river valley. What style of dam might work best in such a spot? An arch dam! Try building your very own arch dam.

The ancient Romans built the world's first known arch dam, Glanum Dam, more than 2,000 years ago.

What You Will Need

- A plastic container approximately 8 x 13 inches (20 x 33 cm)
- About 1 pound (500 g) of modeling clay
- Three craft sticks, cut in half
- A measuring cup
- 2 cups (0.5 L) of water

Kariba Dam is an arch dam on Zambezi River in Africa. Its reservoir, Lake Kariba, holds the most water of any human-made lake in the world.

Step One

Take a clump of clay and roll it into a cylinder a little longer than the width of your plastic container. Roll another cylinder of the same length.

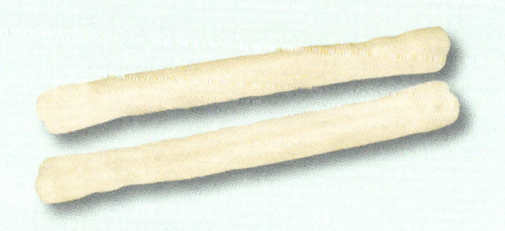

Step Two

Place one cylinder inside the container and form it into an arch shape against the bottom. Stack the other cylinder on top of the first cyclinder. Use your fingers to smooth the cylinders together.

Step Three

Stick the craft sticks into the clay, evenly spaced apart. These will support the rest of the clay and keep it from falling over.

Step Four

Roll more clay cyclinders. Use them to build up a wall against one side of the craft sticks. Make sure there are no gaps. Then, repeat on the other side of the craft sticks.

Step Five

Pour water into the container behind the arch. No water should go through the dam. Success!

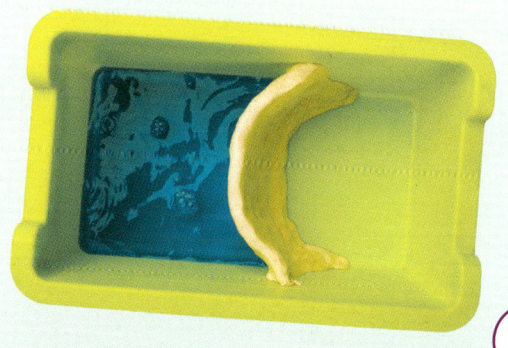

Glossary

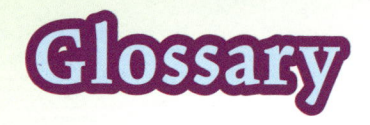

ancient from a long time ago

channel a pathway through which water flows

concrete a hard, strong building material made from sand, gravel, cement, and water

diverted changed the course or pathway of something

engineering the practice of using science and math to design and build structures, machines, and other things people use

environments the natural areas where people and animals live

generator a machine that produces energy

hydroelectric having to do with making energy from flowing water

irrigate to supply with water through a system that is made by humans

locks spaces along waterways with gates at each end used in raising or lowering boats as they pass from level to level

paddle wheels wheels with flat blades that move through water as they turn

population the total number of people living in an area

remote far away from any cities or towns

ruins the remains of a structure that was built long ago

turbine a machine with paddles that is powered by moving water

Read More

Bowman, Chris. *Dams (Blastoff! Readers: Everyday Engineering).* Minneapolis: Bellwether Media, 2019.

Krajnik, Elizabeth. *How a Dam Is Built (Engineering Our World).* New York: Gareth Stevens Publishing, 2020.

Reilly, Kevin. *Dams and Levees (Exploring Infrastructure).* New York: Enslow Publishing, 2019.

Learn More Online

1. Go to **www.factsurfer.com** or scan the QR code below.

2. Enter "**X-Treme Dams**" into the search box.

3. Click on the cover of this book to see a list of websites.

Index

Abu Simbel
  temple complex 18–19

arch dam 8, 16, 24, 28–29

bridges 16

bungee jumping 24–25

buttress dam 8

Colorado River 12, 16–17

concrete 8, 11–14, 16–17, 22, 24

crest 8–9

crocodiles 19

crops 4–5

earthquakes 25

embankment dam 8

flooding 6, 18–19, 24

gravity dam 8, 14, 22

hydroelectric power 5, 9, 13–14,
  19–20, 22

irrigation 4, 6, 19

Lake Mead 12, 17

Lake Nasser 19

Lake Powell 17

Nile River 18–19

paddle wheels 7

Yangtze River 7, 22

About the Author

Catherine C. Finan is a writer living in northeastern Pennsylvania. During a cross-country road trip many years ago, she got to drive across the crest of Hoover Dam.